SAGE ESCAPE
ADULT COLORING BOOK

Cover art and interior illustration by

Damian S Simankowicz

facebook.com/damianssimankowiczart
instagram.com/damianssimankowicz

Published by Primal Archetype. Artwork © Damian S Simankowicz.

ISBN-10: 0-9942549-2-X
ISBN-13: 978-0-9942549-7-9

HOW TO USE THIS BOOK

Time to unwind and take a break from it all.
Grab your tools of choice (color pencils, crayons or markers),
put on your favorite tunes or just enjoy the silence,
and let your creativity take you away!

Choose from simple artwork to more complex pieces based
on your mood. There are dozens of images ranging from
aliens to robots, super soldiers, spaceships and much more!

This book has been created with single sided pages to
help protect your artwork. You can also put a piece of card
behind the image that you are coloring (especially if
you are using markers).

Experiment, there's no one right way, so just have
a good time. Feel free to cut out pages for displaying.
Or even dismantle the book to share with friends.

And most importantly, have fun!

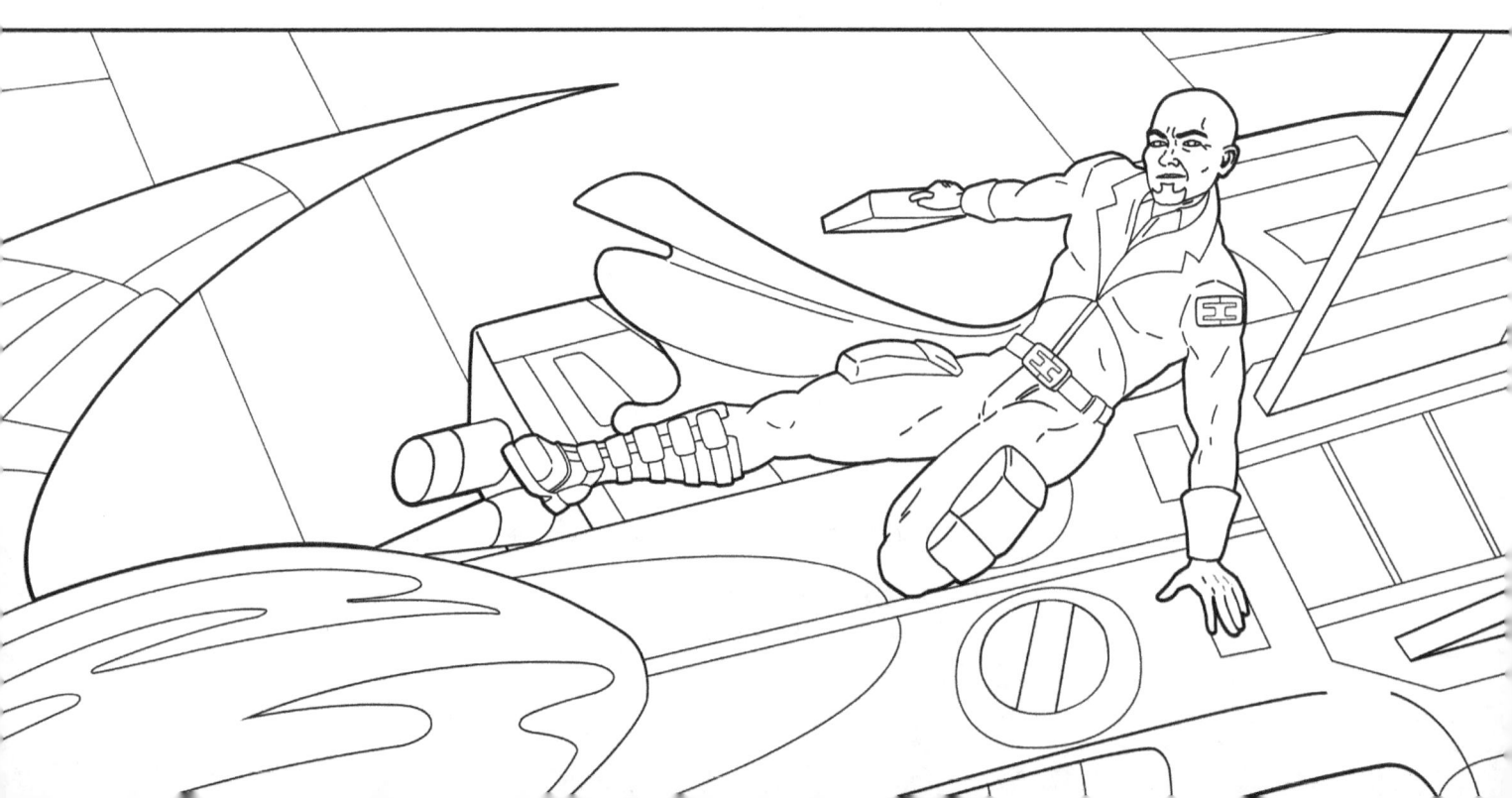

PRACTICE PAGE

Do you have some colors you'd like to try out? Or some techniques?
Or just need to warm up? Here's a page just for that!

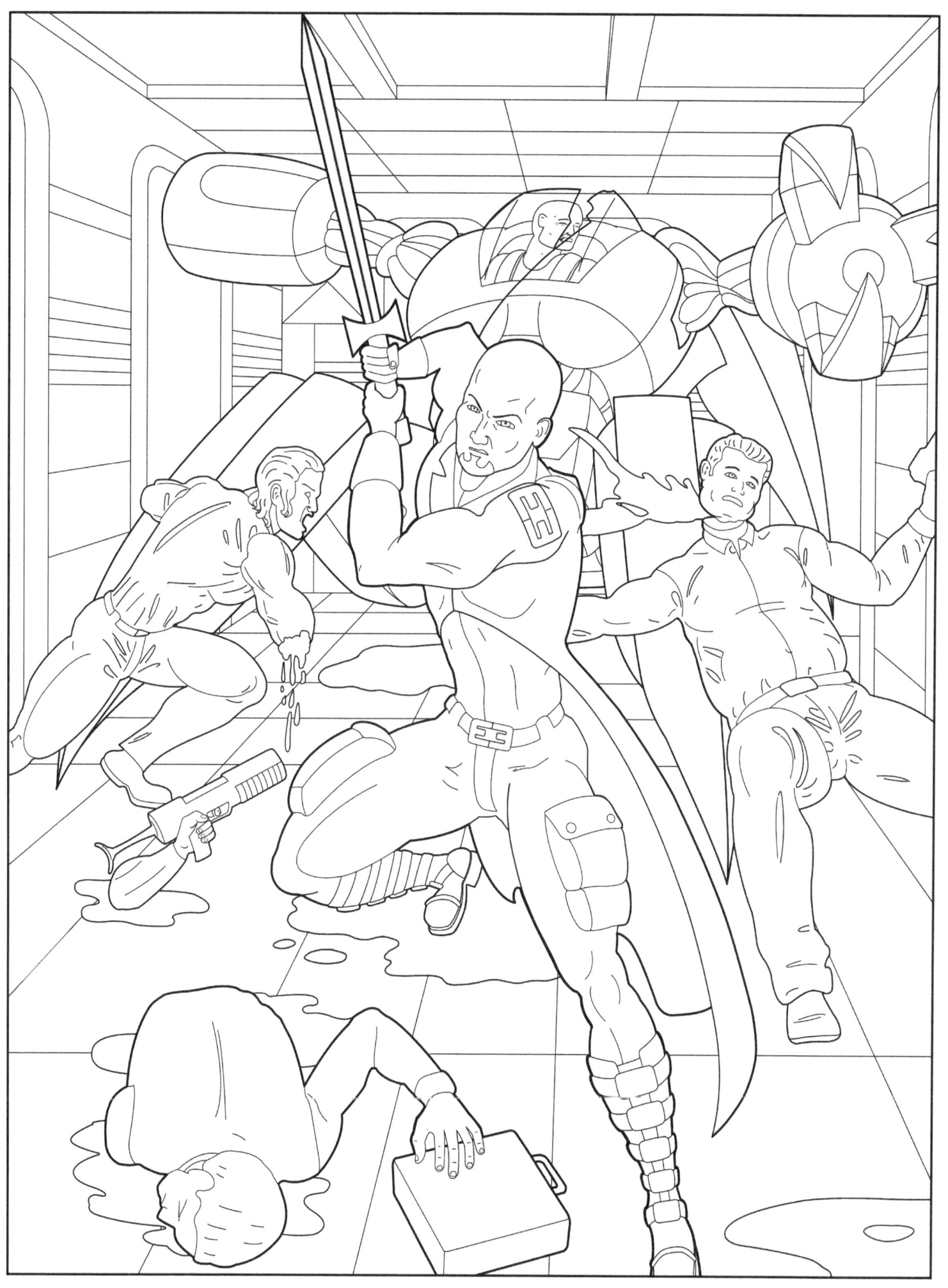

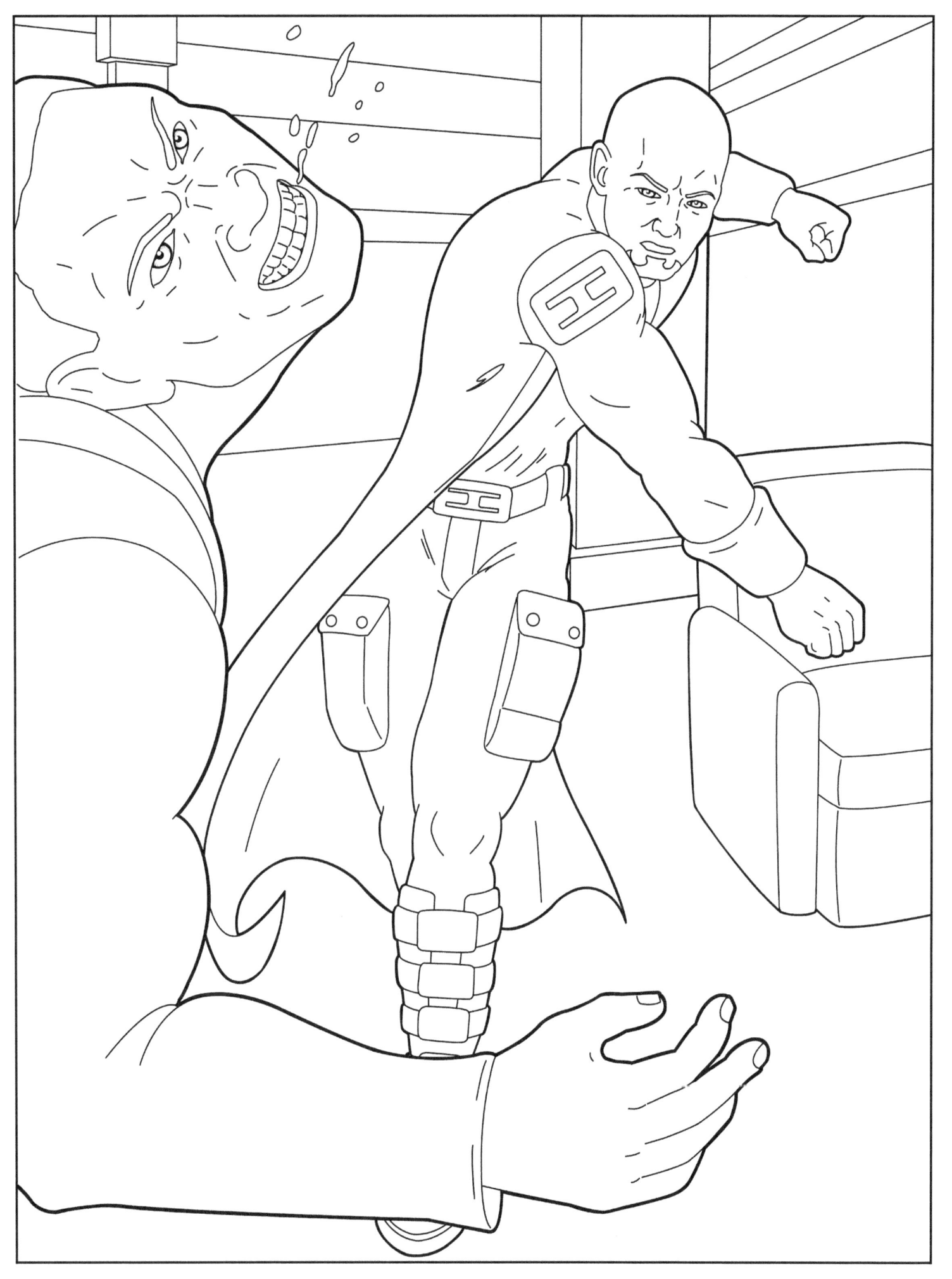

In Memory Of
SAGE

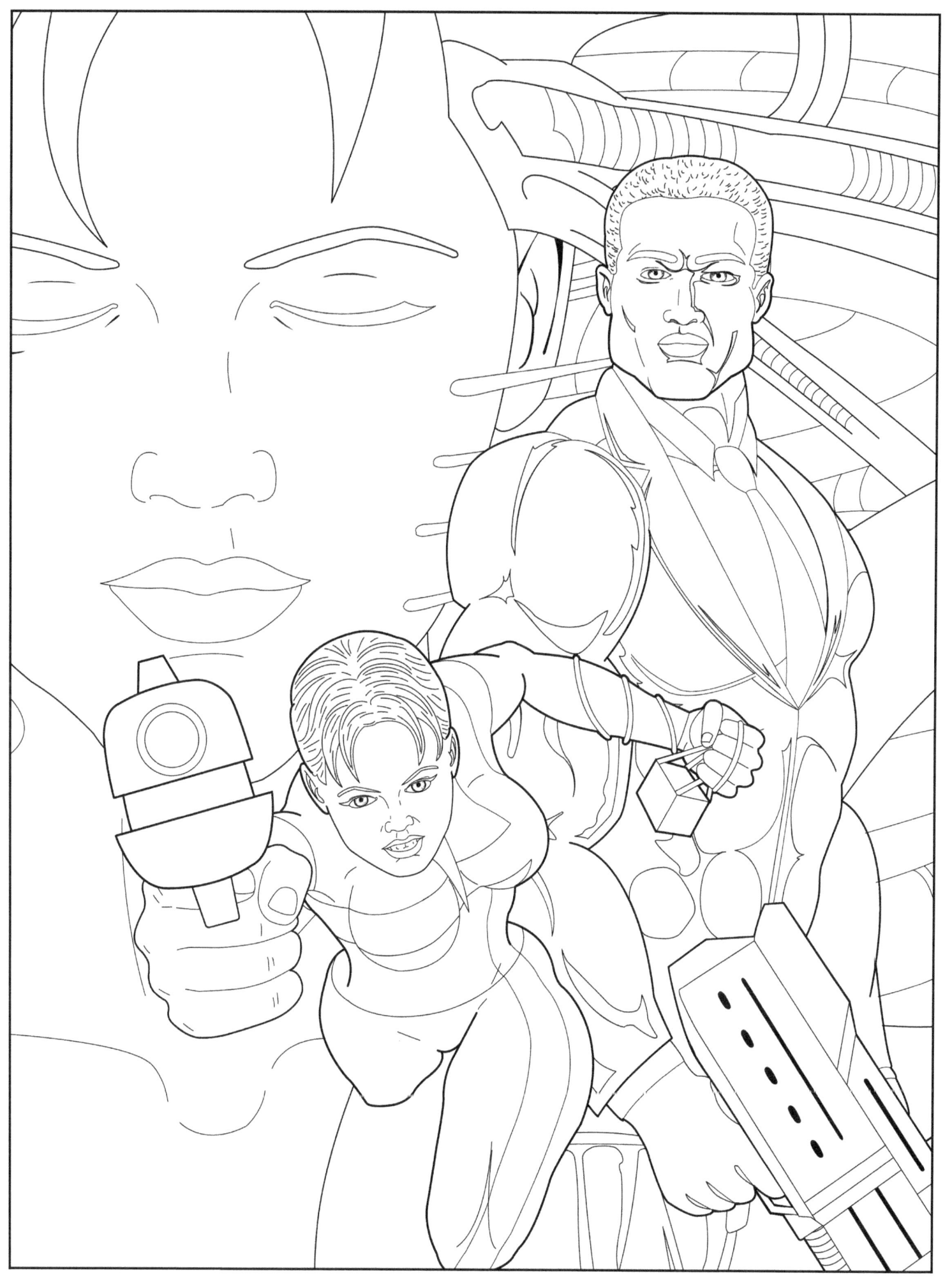

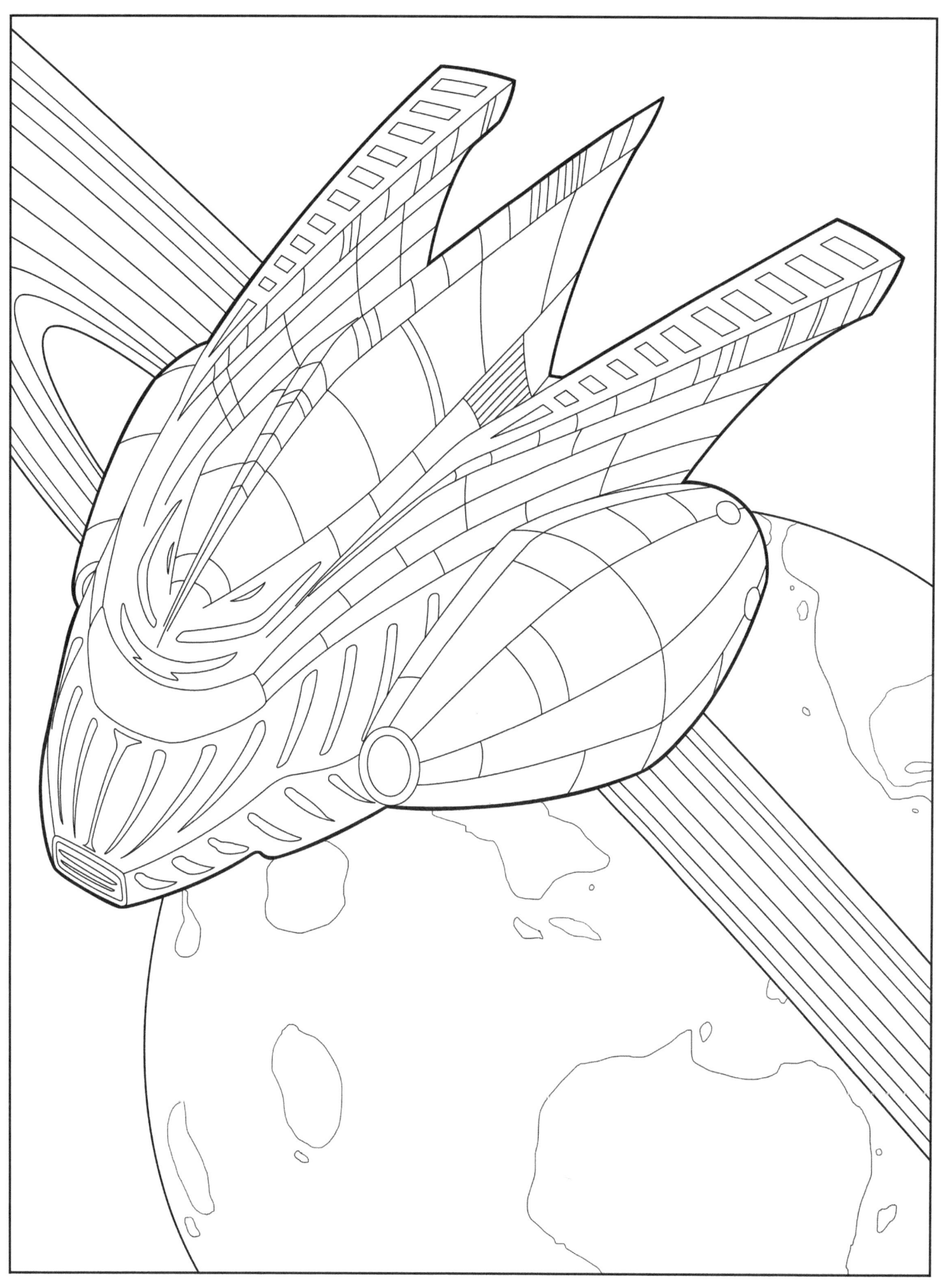

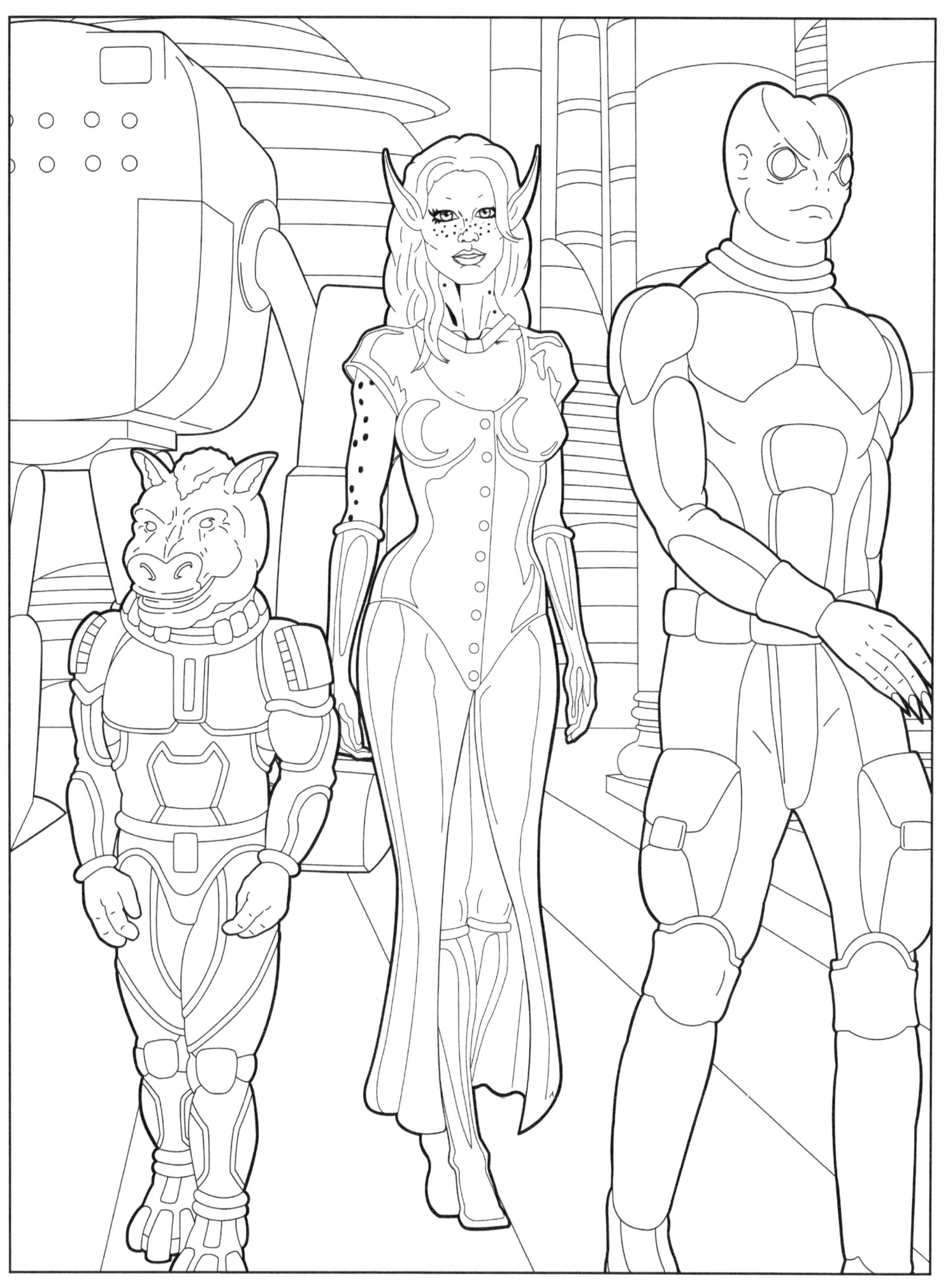

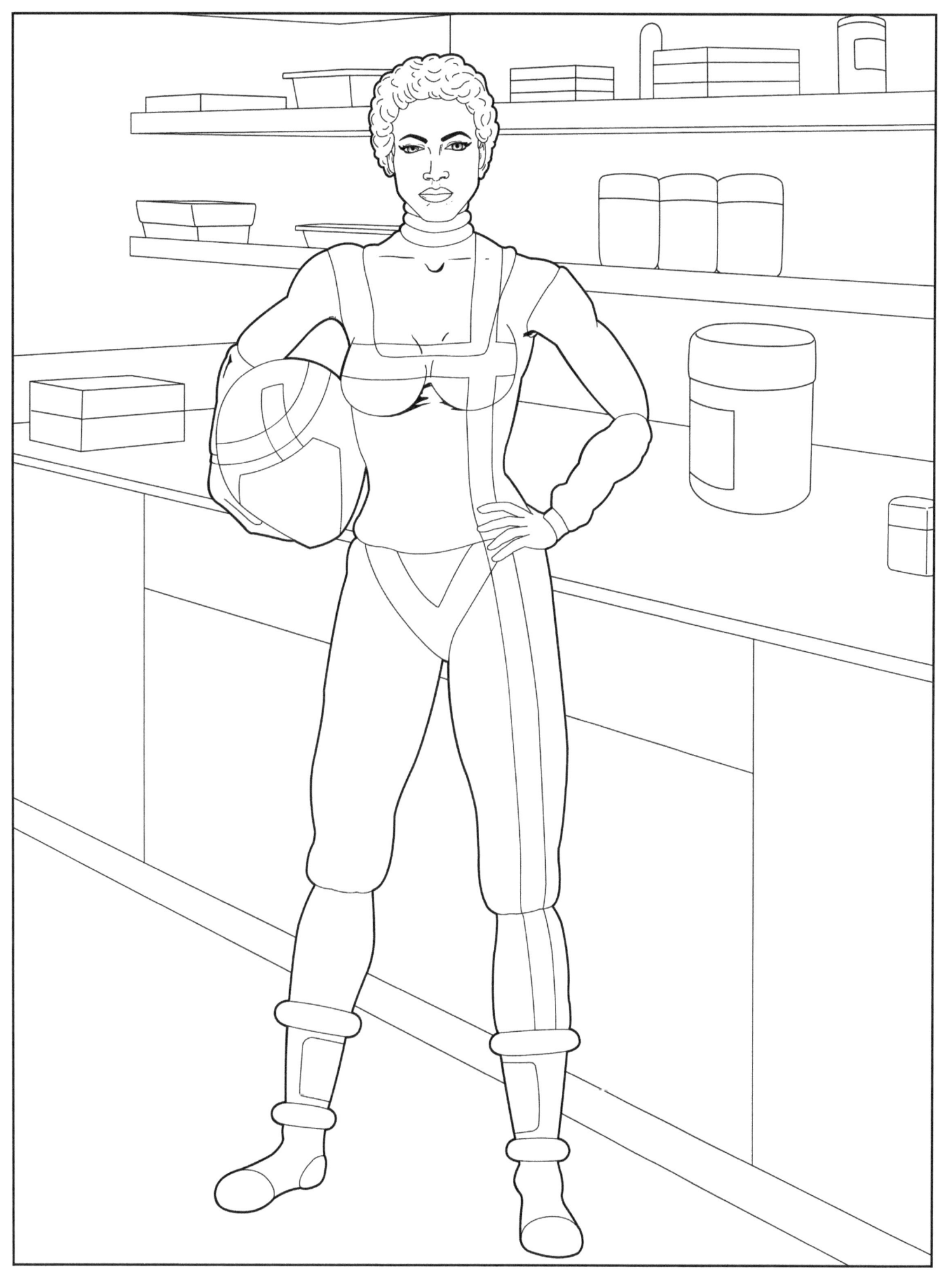

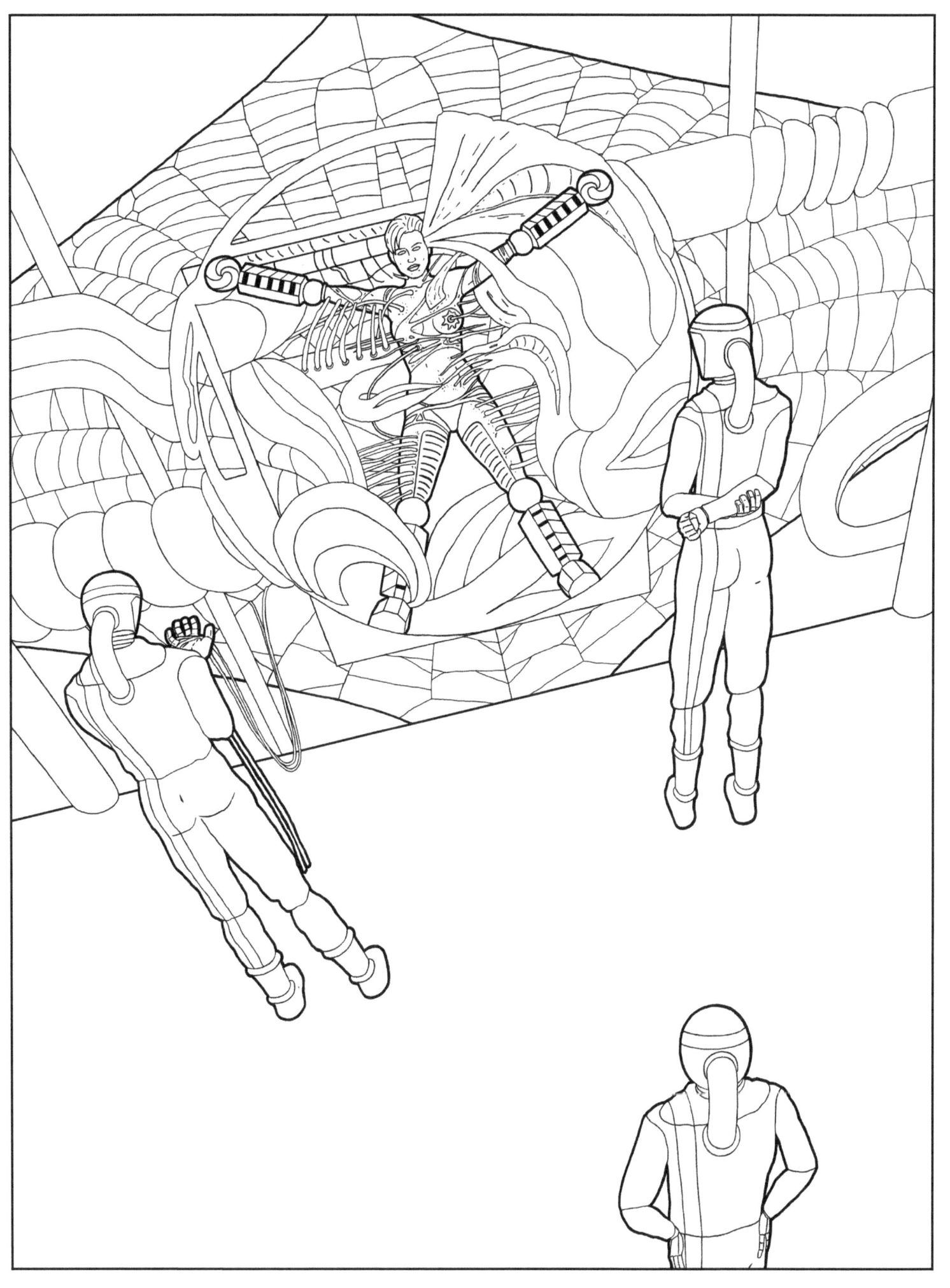

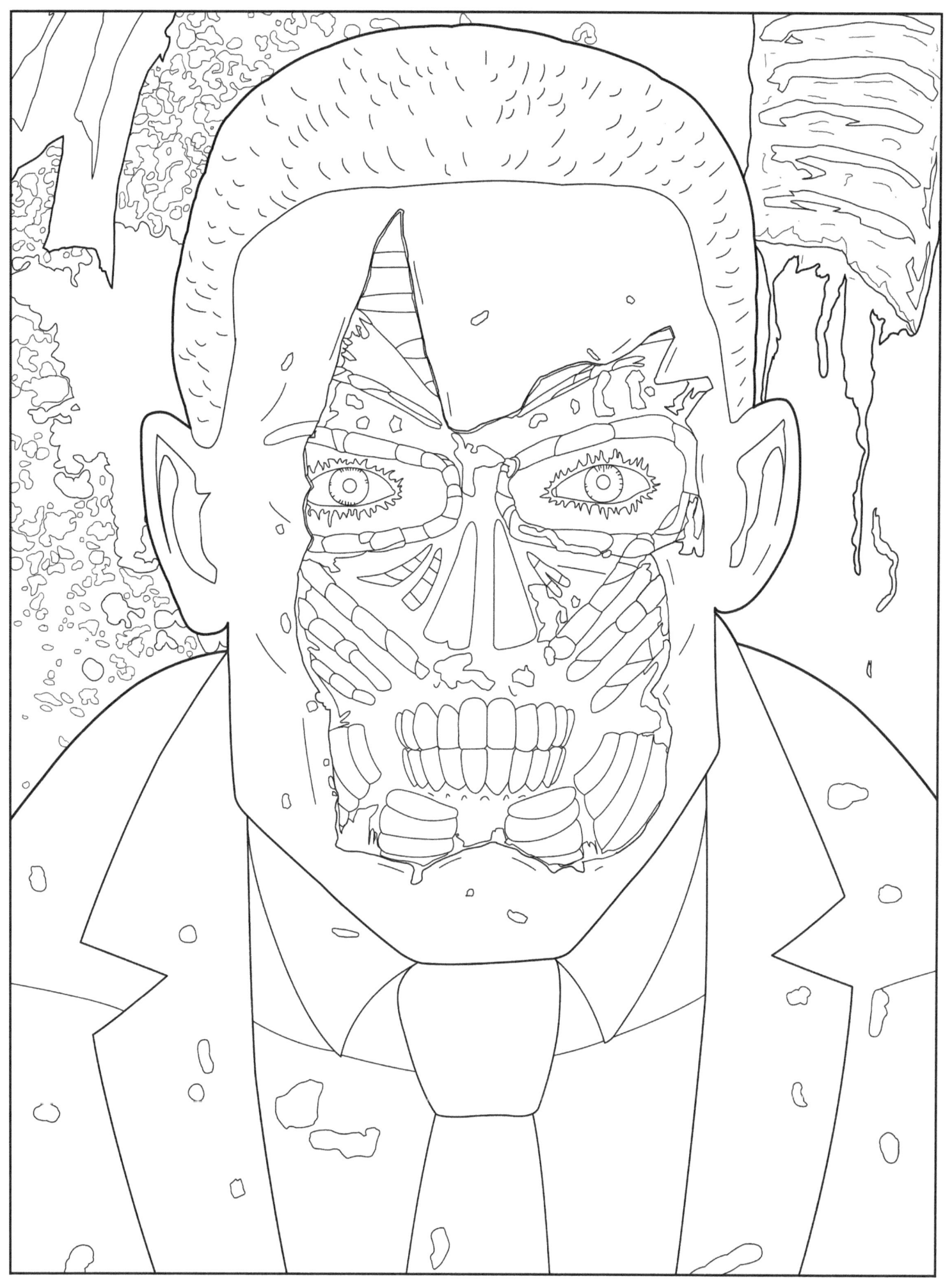

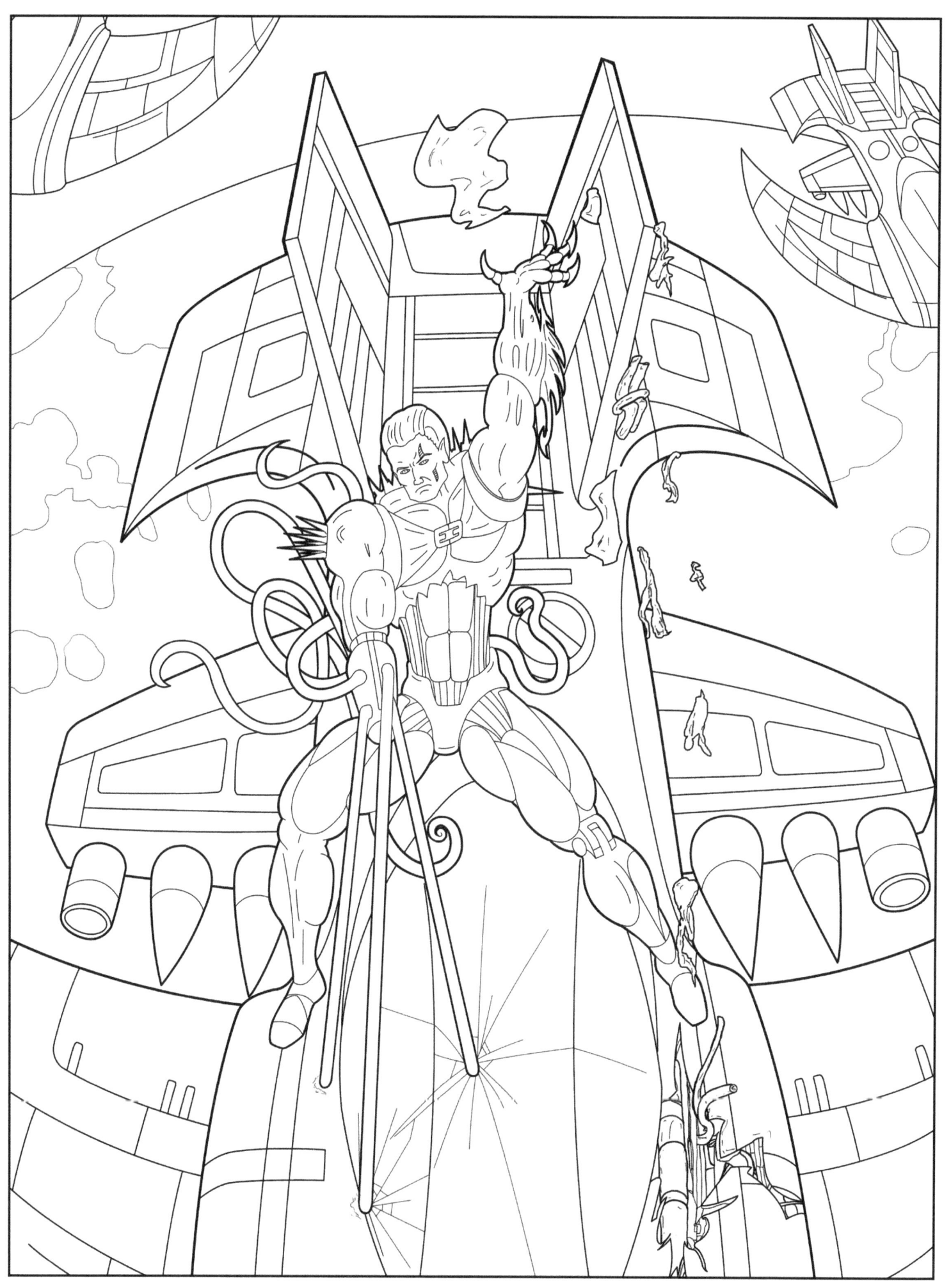

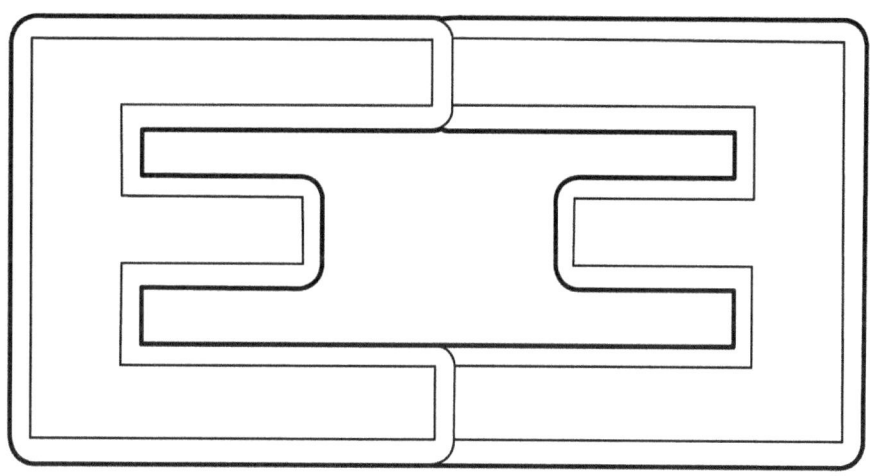